You're All Animals

A Red Fox Book

Published by Random House Children's Books
61-63 Uxbridge Road, London W5 5SA

A division of The Random House Group Ltd
London Melbourne Sydney Auckland
Johannesburg and agencies throughout the world

Copyright © Nicholas Allan 2000

3 5 7 9 10 8 6 4

First published in Great Britain by Hutchinson Children's Books 2000

Red Fox edition 2001

Printed in China

THE RANDOM HOUSE GROUP Limited
Reg. No. 954009

www.kidsatrandomhouse.co.uk

ISBN 9781849417051

NICHOLAS ALLAN

You're All Animals

To Rita

RED FOX

I went to my new school
on Monday.

'This is Billy Trunk,' said Teacher.

Everyone smiled. But I didn't like them.
They were all different.
There was no one like me.

One had teeth all
down his nose...

One was slimy...

One was spotty...   and one smelt
                                      really bad.

I wouldn't talk to any of them.

When I got home I told Mum and Dad.
'I want a friend who's just like me.'

'I know,' said Dad. 'Let's see
if we can find one
on the computer.'

The next day at school I had to do
P.E. with someone with weird arms.

When I got home Dad turned on the computer.

'Wow! Frank sounds just like me!'

So I typed:

The next day at school I had to sit at lunch
with someone who ate strange food
with a dribble-tongue.

I couldn't wait to get home.

'Wow! Frank's just like me!'

So I typed:

The next day at school someone sat down beside me who I thought was really creepy.

When I got home:

So then I typed:

Next morning:

'That Frank is just like me!'

I ran to school. I couldn't wait to meet Frank.
At last I had a friend who was just like me.

When I got there I looked and looked.
I couldn't see Frank anywhere.

But just then I heard a voice
call out, 'Watcha, Billy!'

I turned, and that's when I saw
my great friend Frank, who I already
knew for sure was just like me!